Harbor

Chad Beguelin

A SAMUEL FRENCH ACTING EDITION

FOUNDED 1830

SAMUELFRENCH.COM
SAMUELFRENCH-LONDON.CO.UK

ISBN 978-0-573-70271-6

www.SamuelFrench.com
www.SamuelFrench-London.co.uk

MUSIC USE NOTE

Licensees are solely responsible for obtaining formal written permission from copyright owners to use copyrighted music in the performance of this play and are strongly cautioned to do so. If no such permission is obtained by the licensee, then the licensee must use only original music that the licensee owns and controls. Licensees are solely responsible and liable for all music clearances and shall indemnify the copyright owners of the play(s) and their licensing agent, Samuel French, against any costs, expenses, losses and liabilities arising from the use of music by licensees. Please contact the appropriate music licensing authority in your territory for the rights to any incidental music.

IMPORTANT BILLING AND CREDIT REQUIREMENTS

If you have obtained performance rights to this title, please refer to your licensing agreement for important billing and credit requirements.

HARBOR was originally produced by the Westport Country Playhouse (Mark Lamos, Artistic Director, Michael Ross, Managing Director) in Westport, Connecticut The opening date was September 1, 2012. The performance was directed by Mark Lamos, with sets by Andrew Jackness, costumes by Candice Donnelly, lighting by Japhy Weideman, and original music and sound by John Gromada. The Production Stage Manager was Matthew Melchiorre. The cast was as follows:

DONNA . . . . Kate Nowlin

LOTTIE . . . . Alexis Molnar

KEVIN . . . . Bobby Steggart

TED . . . . .Paul Anthony Stewart

The New York premiere of *HARBOR* was produced by Primary Stages (Casey Childs, Founder & Executive Producer; Andrew Leynse, Artistic Director; Elliot Fox, Managing Director), at 59E59 Theaters. The opening date was August 6, 2013. The performance was directed by Mark Lamos, with sets by Andrew Jackness, costumes by Candice Donnelly, lighting by Japhy Weideman, and original music and sound by John Gromada. The Production Stage Manager was Amanda Spooner. The cast was as follows:

DONNA . . . . Erin Cummings

LOTTIE . . . . Alexis Molnar

KEVIN . . . . Randy Harrison

TED . . . . .Paul Anthony Stewart

CHARACTERS

DONNA ADAMS . . . . .mid-thirties, but acts like a teenager

LOTTIE ADAMS . . . . fifteen and a half and acts like an adult

KEVIN ADAMS-WELLER . . . . early thirties, **DONNA**'s brother

TED ADAMS-WELLER. . . . . .late thirties, **KEVIN**'s husband

SETTING

The play takes place over three months in Sag Harbor.

ACT ONE

Scene One

*(A van. **DONNA**, mid-thirties, wishes she were younger, drives. She is sloppily put together, but tries her best to look young in a sadly cool teenager kind of way. **LOTTIE**, 15 and a half, wishes she were older, sits shotgun. **LOTTIE** is dressed much more conservatively than her mother and reads a tattered book. Music blares. **DONNA** turns the music down.)*

DONNA. They hyphenated their last names. Freaking hyphenated them. How gay is that?

LOTTIE. They are gay.

DONNA. Yeah? Well, they just got a lot gayer.

LOTTIE. Um, no. It's actually very straight of them. It's something that straight people do.

DONNA. Yeah, retarded straight people. And of course they'd have to live someplace like this. I mean look at this crap. All these little old time-y shops and windmills. This whole town is just trying too hard. We get it, Sag Harbor. You're cute. It's like "the lady doth deny too much."

LOTTIE. Protest. It's "the lady doth protest too much."

DONNA. Whateves.

*(Punches **LOTTIE** in the shoulder.)*

Slug bug!

LOTTIE. Stop it. Don't you even care when you sound like an idiot?

DONNA. Don't be a dick.

LOTTIE. Don't call me a dick. You can't call me a dick.

DONNA. I'm sorry. Mommy's sorry. Mommy's just stressed out right now. I haven't ever met this Ted person. I want him think I'm cool.

LOTTIE. But you're not cool.

DONNA. I am too! I'm a cool person. People think I'm cool.

LOTTIE. What people? I'd like to meet those people.

DONNA. Come on, don't be a bioatch.

LOTTIE. Don't say that word like that. You're too old to say that word like that.

DONNA. I'm not old. I'm down. I represent.

LOTTIE. No one talks like that anymore. Please don't talk like that in front of them.

DONNA. Oh, look. A store that sells salt water taffy. Welcome to Fag Harbor.

LOTTIE. *(Shaking her head.)* So not cool.

DONNA What are you reading now?

(Grabs the book.)

"House of Mirth"? Is it funny?

LOTTIE. It's hilarious.

DONNA. What's it about?

LOTTIE. Lily Bart. She's a milliner who's hooked on chloral hydrate.

DONNA. In English, please?

LOTTIE. She's a drug addict who makes hats.

DONNA. Oh.

LOTTIE. She blew all her chances to settle down. Scared all the men in her life away.

DONNA. What's that supposed to mean?

LOTTIE. I'm just telling you about the book.

DONNA. I still can't believe Kevin's married now. I wonder if he's going to call this Ted person his husband

LOTTIE. What did he call him when you spoke to him? Did he say "husband"?

DONNA. *(Shrugs it off.)* I dunno.

LOTTIE. When was the last time you talked to Uncle Kevin?

DONNA. I don't know. Why you gotta be like that, bioatch?

LOTTIE. I said don't. They know we're coming, right?

*(**DONNA** is silent.)*

Mom?!

*(Lights up on a meticulously restored Greek Revival living room. **KEVIN**, sensitive and easily rattled, sits at a Biedermeier writing desk, pounding away at his laptop.)*

KEVIN. *(Stops typing, then throws his head back in disgust.)* Oh my God, just stab me in the back of the head! Just find a soft spot in my skull and stick a knife through it!

TED. *(Offstage.)* Don't make yourself crazy.

KEVIN. It's total crap.

TED. *(Offstage.)* Read me what you've got.

KEVIN. Where's my coffee?

TED. *(Offstage.)* It's coming, bossy. Read.

KEVIN. *(Sighs, reads.)* Originally called Wigwagonock by local Native Americans, Sag Harbor rests on a peaceful bay in the heart of the Hamptons. From the Bay Street Gala to the Hampton Classic Horse Show, Sag Harbor offers its citizens and visitors alike a wide array of exciting activities…

*(**TED** enters with coffee, seemingly unflappable.)*

TED. That's good. What's wrong with that?

KEVIN. That doesn't sound wooden to you? Professorial?

TED. It flows. It's informational. It has a kind of singleness of purpose.

KEVIN. I hate you.

(Goes back to typing. Stops abruptly.)

It's just humiliating. I'm going to tell them I can't do it.

TED. No you're not. It was very nice of Anne and Vivian to ask you to help. They know you want to be a writer…

(Quickly corrects himself.)

That you <u>are</u> a writer and I think it's a great opportunity.

KEVIN. It's just a pamphlet.

TED. So you should be able to bang it out in no time.

KEVIN. *(Sips coffee.)* I wish this coffee was more ethnic.

TED. Mexican or Irish?

KEVIN. Irish.

*(**TED** crosses to a bar and grabs some whiskey. He pours it into their cups.)*

Maybe I just have to leave it for now. Pick it up tomorrow, when I've got more perspective. Maybe I should walk around town and pick up some inspiration.

TED. Why don't you finish your homework first, young man?

KEVIN. You're right. You think I'm just procrastinating? Trying to distract myself? Can we get a dog?

TED. No.

KEVIN. A little one?

TED. No.

KEVIN. A picture of a dog?

TED. No.

*(Lights switch to **DONNA** and **LOTTIE**.)*

DONNA. Look for number 32.

LOTTIE. How could you not tell them we were coming? I can't believe how stupid you are.

DONNA. Don't worry about it. Kevin worships me. And I'm sure they'll have about a thousand bedrooms, so why would they care?

LOTTIE. Are they gonna have a computer?

DONNA. Are you kidding? They'll have a computer that makes cappuccinos and gives blowjobs. Trust me, everything is going to be over the top and we're gonna be very jealous. But just be cool about it.

(Pause.)

Why do you want a computer?

LOTTIE. I want to email someone.

DONNA. Leave Jim alone, Lottie. It's not cool.

LOTTIE. He's my dad. I can email whomever I want.

DONNA. You'll just annoy him.

LOTTIE. You don't know that.

DONNA. Has he emailed you back in four years?

LOTTIE. Forget it.

DONNA. Look for numbers.

LOTTIE. 28…30…there it is, turn here.

DONNA. Oh…oh, shit…

(Pulls the van to a stop.)

Look at it.

LOTTIE. Um…wow.

DONNA. *(Starts to cry.)* It looks like a wedding cake.

LOTTIE. What is wrong with you?

DONNA. What do you think is wrong with me?! Your uncle lives in a wedding cake with a hyphenated last name and I live with you in a van.

(Pounds the steering wheel.)

We live in a fucking van!

LOTTIE. Stop it! You're gonna break the steering wheel! Then we're gonna live in a van with a broken steering wheel.

DONNA. I should just kill myself!

LOTTIE. Don't say that! You can't say that!

DONNA. Oh, come on! Don't tell me you wouldn't be better off! You'd probably get to live with your gay uncles and they'd French braid your hair and pack you lunches with little plastic containers of chicken salad…and desserts. There'd always be some kind of fancy dessert. Tarts.

LOTTIE. Shut up right now.

DONNA. I should have married that hotel manager in Louisville. Everyone else settles, why didn't I? Why am I any better than the rest of America? Why can't I just overlook people's downfalls? So he had a cleft lip. Big deal. I could have thought of it as just another way to show off what great teeth he had. It's just the stomach that hung over the belt. I can't lift up a stomach before I have sex with someone, Lottie. I can't do that.

LOTTIE. No one's asking you to. Am I asking you to?

(Pause.)

Look at your face.

DONNA. *(Checks her reflection.)* Oh God. It looks like I put my make-up on with the butt of a gun.

LOTTIE. Let me fix it.

*(**LOTTIE** starts to redo **DONNA**'s make-up.)*

DONNA. You're the world to me, baby. I love you.

LOTTIE. Whatever.

DONNA. No, I mean it.

LOTTIE. Um, noted. Why don't you call them first? Let's go back to the gas station and call them. It'll make it all just, you know, easier.

DONNA. You're right. Let's make this whole thing much more chill.

(Starts the car.)

Can I smoke just a little weed before I call?

LOTTIE. No.

DONNA. Just a teeny tiny bit? Just to calm my nerves?

LOTTIE Absolutely not.

DONNA. You're a mean mommy.

*(Lights switch to **TED** and **KEVIN**. **TED** is now typing and **KEVIN** paces.)*

KEVIN. What have you got?

TED. This is a rough draft.

(Reads)

Evidence of Sag Harbor's history as a whaling port can be found in the light blue curbstones used along the city streets. The curbstones were fashioned out of the ballasts of ancient whaling ships that frequented the port.

KEVIN. That's not bad. You're better than me.

TED. Come on, baby. You're an artist. I'm an architect.

KEVIN. Then why are words just flowing out of you?

TED. This is non-fiction. I'm just…building sentences. There's no creativity.

KEVIN. I'm a hack.

TED. Forget it. I'll cut the whole paragraph.

KEVIN. No, it's fine. Leave it. Maybe I'll try and design a few office buildings. See how you like it.

(The phone rings.)

TED. Don't be like that. I'm just trying to help.

KEVIN. *(Loudly, annoyed.)* I know that! You think I don't know that?!

(Instantly switching to calm as he answers the phone.)

Adams-Weller residence.

(A light comes up on **DONNA** *at a payphone.)*

DONNA. Hey, Kevin? It's Donna. Is this a bad time?

KEVIN. *(Thrown)* Oh, hey…hey, you. Long time no talk… so…no, it's not a bad, is everything okay?

DONNA. Oh, everything's great. Really awesome.

KEVIN. Lottie's okay? Everyone's okay?

DONNA. Yeah, um, super okay. Everyone's really awesome and filled with…super okay-ness. Hey, guess where I'm calling you from!

KEVIN. Um, I don't know. Dollywood?

DONNA. No, I – what? No, think, Kevin!

KEVIN. Oh, God. You're not calling from jail, are you?

DONNA. Ha! That's funny! No, ha! No, I'm like, three blocks away.

KEVIN. Three blocks away from what?

DONNA. From, you know, you. You two. You two guys.

TED. Who is it?

KEVIN. *(To* **TED***)* Shhh!

DONNA. If now's a bad time…

KEVIN. Uh, no, why would it be? I'm just, Ted and I were just, I was just doing some work, some writing…and we're having coffee and I was…you know, writing… and…so that's what we're doing…in a nutshell. In the shell of a…nut…

DONNA. I'm at a gas station three blocks away.

KEVIN. That's so crazy. Three blocks huh?

(After a brutally long pause.)

DONNA. So, um, Kevin?

KEVIN. Yeah?

DONNA. Are you gonna invite me over?

KEVIN. Well, um…that's…that's exactly what I'm going to do.

(Blackout.)

Scene Two

(Minutes later. **LOTTIE**, **DONNA**, **KEVIN** *and* **TED** *sit very awkwardly in the living room. There are several large, worn looking backpacks piled to one side.)*

KEVIN. Lottie is so big. She's just grown so much.

DONNA. Fifteen going on forty. She's always been mature for her age. Got her period when she was ten.

LOTTIE. Oh my God, shut up!

KEVIN. Yeah, that's probably not appropriate.

DONNA. Oh, Lottie gets me. I'm a dope mom. She thinks I'm dope.

LOTTIE. No, I don't. I think you're a moron.

TED. Wow.

DONNA. Hey, Ted, I don't mean to be a bitch, but can we get something to drink?

TED. Oh, Jesus, sorry. What would you like? Wine? Vodka? Beer? We're prepared for anything.

DONNA. Whatever you're drinking. What are you drinking?

TED. We were just having plain old coffee, but I could shake up some vodka martinis if…

DONNA. Fuck yeah!

TED. I'll just be right the fuck back.

*(*TED *is gone.)*

DONNA. He's fun.

KEVIN. Yeah.

DONNA. He's so glossy and satisfied.

KEVIN. I guess. So, last I heard you were all the way out in San Francisco…

DONNA. Yeah, I was singing with this band, you know, weddings and bar mitzvahs…a few hotel conventions…

LOTTIE. A car show.

DONNA. A car show. And it just started to kill me on the inside, you know what I mean? I could feel my organs rotting. The money was fine, nothing great, but the crap I had to sing.

LOTTIE. Bryan Adams.

DONNA. Bryan freaking Adams! Talk about torture! I mean, who gets married to Bryan freaking Adams?

LOTTIE. Hillbillies.

DONNA. Hillbillies! And the brides would stand there and cry, never realizing that they haven't gotten married, they've just been sold into slavery. I mean, in my book, all relationships are just two-person cults.

(*Quick pause.*)

Present company excluded, of course.

KEVIN. Of course.

DONNA. So, you know, it wasn't a choice, I had to quit.

LOTTIE. They fired you.

DONNA. I quit, Lottie. My decision.

LOTTIE. She exposed her breasts.

DONNA. Accidentally.

LOTTIE. And hit on one of the grooms.

DONNA. That was technically before the wedding, so I deflect all evil karma.

LOTTIE. She stole a Rabbi's wallet.

DONNA. (*To* **LOTTIE**) Do I interrupt your stories?

LOTTIE. I don't have any stories.

KEVIN. Hey, Lottie. So, uh, where do you go to school?

DONNA. She's kind of home-schooled.

LOTTIE. We live in a van.

DONNA. So you're van-schooled.

(**TED** *returns with a shaker. He pours drinks for* **KEVIN** *and* **DONNA**.)

She makes such a big deal about crashing in the van every now and then. I mean, Jewel lived out of her car and now she's got platinum albums and shit.

(**DONNA** *addresses* **TED**.)

DONNA. Lottie likes juice and those cheddar goldfish crackers. Or cheese? You got cheese?

*(**TED** stares at her.)*

Or Snackables?

*(**TED** shoots **KEVIN** a look.)*

KEVIN. Let me help.

TED. No, no. I'm good.

(He turns and exits.)

DONNA. *(Back to **KEVIN**.)* He's great. So this guy who used to play the synthesizer tells me he's quitting the band, too, but that his brother works for a cruise ship that leaves out of New York. His brother got him a gig on the boat and he thinks he can hook me up with an audition. I mean, it's not exactly what I had in mind for my singing career, but you can make some sweet money. He claims it's somewhere around thirty thousand a year, plus your room and board are all taken care of. Thirty thousand? That's almost a double wide trailer after taxes. Lottie and I would be all set. So we decide to head east and then I realize you're out here and you haven't seen Lottie since God knows when…

KEVIN. I think it was mom's funeral.

DONNA. I knew it was some kind of joyous occasion. So I figured we had to stop by.

KEVIN. Well, it's great. I mean, it's such a surprise.

DONNA. I know, isn't this fun?! So, I wanna hear all about you! All about you and Ted and this great house and everything that's going on in Kevin-Ted world. How long have you two been together?

KEVIN. Coming up on ten years.

DONNA. Whoa, that's almost fifty-three in straight people years.

KEVIN. Is it?

DONNA. I interrupted. What have you been up to, bro?

KEVIN. Well, I've been working on some projects. A novel that I'm wrestling with right now. It's going slowly, but I'll get there. I'll get there.

DONNA. You'll have to let me read it!

(To **LOTTIE***)*

Uncle Kevin's the only one that went to college. Full scholarship. Superior to all of us in every way. Straight A's. Straight teeth. Straight throw pillows. Take a cue from your uncle, bioatch.

(To **KEVIN***)*

She's gonna be just like you. Spitting image.

KEVIN. You like to read, Lottie?

LOTTIE. What's the book about?

KEVIN. What's it about? Oh, it's you know, it's kind of hard to explain. It's about this woman, well, the voice is very female…

DONNA. Of course it is.

KEVIN. It's…it's, well, in a way, it's sort of a cross between… it's kind of like…I mean, she wakes up…

LOTTIE. The woman?

KEVIN. Yes, it's all kind of…visceral…and you don't know if you can trust her narration, because it might be so esoteric that it's apocryphal.

DONNA. I don't know what any of those words mean.

KEVIN. It's hard to explain. I'm struggling, but…

DONNA. You should put some vampires in it.

KEVIN. What? It's not that kind of…why would I do that?

DONNA. Everybody's making mad money off of vampire shit. Or zombies.

KEVIN. Sorry, Donna, but, what kind of books do you read?

DONNA. Me? Oh, I'm a magazine girl. But that doesn't mean I don't know what sells. I've got my finger on the pulse.

KEVIN. Right.

(Quickly.)

I'm also working on a pamphlet. For the historical society.

DONNA. Oh. Is that good? I mean, that's good.

KEVIN. There are a lot of writers out here. They have a writers' conference every summer. They could have asked anybody to do it. Somebody big.

TED. *(Re-enters with a tray.)* They could have asked E.L. Doctorow.

KEVIN. Well, not that big.

DONNA. But instead they asked you! Wow, well, hey! Cheers!

(To **LOTTIE.***)*

You hear that? Your uncle's writing a famous pamphlet. Eat something, Lottie.

(Picks up a cornichon.)

Try one of these shrunken pickles.

KEVIN. They're cornichons.

DONNA. Well, la-de-da!

LOTTIE. I'm not hungry. Can I use your bathroom?

TED. Down the hall, to the right.

LOTTIE. *(Stops, to* **KEVIN.***)* Your book sounds a lot like "Mrs. Dalloway". You know, by Virginia Woolf. It's very stream of consciousness, too. She's stuck in what they call a kind of "continuous present." Events keep moving around in her mind, so you're not sure you can trust her narration either. You know, like your book.

KEVIN. *(Pause.)* Huh. I'll have to pick that up again. You've…you've read Virginia Woolf?

LOTTIE. Yeah, well, classics are only a quarter at the Goodwill. Less if the cover's ripped off.

*(***LOTTIE*** exits.)*

KEVIN. Jesus. She's read Virginia Woolf?

DONNA. I told you she's wicked smart. She's like, Asian smart. Is that racist? I guess it's not racist if it's a compliment, right? I mean, if someone said all fags have huge dicks, you guys wouldn't get pissed off, right?

TED. I'm gonna need some time to think about that.

DONNA. So, Ted, what's kind of stuff do you design?

TED. Well, I was sort of forced into residential when the market went south. I used to do a lot more commercial work, that's where my passion is.

KEVIN. You should see the library that Ted designed a few years ago. It's been Leed Certified.

DONNA. Awesome. What the hell's that?

TED. It stands for Leadership in Energy and Environmental Design. It just basically means, you know, the building is up to the standards of the US Green Building Council.

KEVIN. It's an earth friendly design, uses sustainable energy...

TED. Blah, blah, blah.

DONNA. Wow, so it's really noble, then.

TED. Well, I don't know about that. There's a little bit of nobility somewhere maybe, but it's also the way things are going. I'm just doing what the market demands.

DONNA. But it's not like you're building rape rooms.

TED. Uh...no.

KEVIN. Ted's had two buildings certified at the gold level. They do different levels, silver, gold, platinum.

DONNA. Sounds like Amway. That's cute how you do that. Brag about each other. It's cute. Super supportive and shit. You guys ever think about adopting some kids? Maybe do the surrogate thing?

TED. *(Pause.)* How did my glass get so empty?

(He shakes the martini shaker vigorously. Pours himself a drink. Motions to **KEVIN***'s glass.)*

KEVIN. I'm okay for now.

DONNA. I'm not.

(Holds her glass up to be filled.)

So no babies for you two?

KEVIN. Ted hates babies. He thinks all babies should be baked into pies.

TED. That's not true. I just, I don't think we're the type of people. We're too selfish.

KEVIN. We're not!

TED. Yes, baby, we are. We like to travel and shop and booze it up. If it were a choice between a week at a swim-up bar in St. Kitts or diapers, I'd have to say screw the diapers. I guess, you know, it's just, it's never been a priority.

DONNA. Oh, come on, now! How could you not want kids? I mean, you've got the fancy house, the hyphenated names. Wouldn't a kid be the next logical step for you two upstanding Gay-mericans?

TED. I'm just not into the whole big family thing. And neither is Kevin.

DONNA. You're not? When we were kids…

KEVIN. That's all changed.

DONNA. *(To TED.)* When we were kids, Kevin would force me to play house. I would have to pretend to be his daughter. And he would pretend to be the mommy.

KEVIN. Oh, God, shut up.

DONNA. He would wear bright orange dish washing gloves and constantly lecture me about manners. And he used this high-class southern accent, like Dinah Shore.

KEVIN. *(With a southern accent.)* Young lady, what have I told you about acting up in front of company?

DONNA. *(With the same accent.)* Where, pray tell, are your pantyhose?

KEVIN & DONNA. *(With the accent.)* That is not the proper way to use an oyster fork!

(They laugh together for a second.)

KEVIN. Yeah, well...

(Pause.)

We had the chance. Once. A lesbian couple we know asked if I would donate my, you know...my...

DONNA. Your splooge?

KEVIN. Uh, sure. They wanted a second kid. They adopted the first time around, a beautiful girl. Trina. But this time they wanted me to...we talked about it, but you know, it wasn't really a good idea. The kid would ultimately be their kid and not ours. Not that we actually wanted..you know...

TED. *(To* KEVIN.*)* Anne and Vivian are very happy with the way things turned out.

KEVIN. They ended up going through a sperm bank. You should see their kids. They couldn't be more perfect. Little matchy-matchy outfits. Like someone shook them out of a J. Crew catalogue.

DONNA. Someone sounds jealous.

KEVIN. What? No!

TED. I'm surprised either of you would want to have kids after the childhood Kevin's described.

DONNA. What did you tell him?

TED. The alcoholic mother, the verbal abuse, it makes "Angela's Ashes" look like musical comedy.

DONNA. Kevin exaggerates.

KEVIN. It's too bad, because Ted would make a really great father.

TED. Okay, let's just drop it.

DONNA. You would, Ted. You would make a fucking awesome dad.

TED. No, I wouldn't! I wouldn't because, I just...I hate that everyone has to make me feel so guilty about the kid thing.

DONNA. But kids are great! I'd die if I didn't have Lottie.

TED. Well, that's great. For you. That's a personal life choice that you made and I'm happy for you. But I am not gonna feel guilty.

DONNA. But what about what Kevin wants?

KEVIN. I want what Ted wants. I mean, we want the same thing. The same things.

DONNA. But kids are great! What's not to like about kids?

TED. Everything! Okay, I just…when did all of this happen? Why are all of our friends pressuring us to have kids? One of the best benefits of being gay, aside from the really great taste in window treatments, is that kids aren't expected to be part of the equation. When did that change? Anne and Vivian, the two Bobs…

DONNA. You have two gay friends named Bob? As in the gaybobs? That's hilarious.

TED. *(Pouring what's left of the shaker into his glass.)* And I especially don't want to turn into those people. Those entitled parents. I can't stand them. With their double-wide strollers that take up the entire sidewalk. And they way they let their babies scream for hours in restaurants like the rest of us should act like we don't hear them. Like we've all gone spontaneously deaf. Or the way they think they should go first in lines at the airport or the supermarket or anywhere else on the planet because they're so special because they're carrying a baby. "Oh, watch out for the baby! Make way for the baby! Precious, precious baby comes first!" I just want to say to them, "I don't care about your baby. I didn't ask you to have a baby. And I certainly don't see why the world should just move aside because you decided to spread your legs like a five cent whore one night!"

DONNA. Whoa! I wasn't expecting that.

KEVIN. Ted, Jesus. Let's not…

TED. Sorry, you're right. Let's just drop it! I mean, enough with the entitled mothers! I'm done. I'm sorry.

(Pause.)

But you know which ones are the worst? The ones that are always trying to push their babies on you. Hold the baby, kiss the baby, worship the baby. Well, guess what? I don't want to see your baby. I don't want to get near your filthy, dirty baby. You know what babies are? They're Petri dishes, full of bacteria and snot and noise and I chose a life far away from them and yet everyone I know keeps trying to shove them down my throat.

KEVIN. No one's trying to shove anything down you're throat.

(To **DONNA.***)*

He goes on these tirades.

DONNA. No shit.

TED. I'm sorry, I'm sorry. I'm not gonna say another word.

(Pause.)

But you know what's really scary? The fact that nobody has just one baby these days. Thanks to modern medicine, everyone's got three, four, five babies. Remember when we were kids and someone would have a twin and it was scary and strange, like a leprechaun or a unicorn or a leprechaun riding a unicorn? But not anymore! The whole thing has gotten so crazy. And these entitled people just bring up even more entitled children! I can't even design a normal house anymore. I've got to design a master bathroom inside a master bathroom because my female clients have to urinate twenty-four hours a day because they've got fifty-three babies growing inside of them. So, are we gonna have kids, no God damn way!

*(***LOTTIE*** enters, unseen by* **TED.***)*

Because kids ruin your life and I have yet to meet a kid who is not a complete and total buzz kill!

(He turns to see **LOTTIE.** *Without missing a beat he tries to snap on a forced cheeriness.)*

Except for Lottie! Hi, Lottie, would you like more cheese? I'll get you more cheese! Lottie needs cheese!

(He grabs the tray and beelines offstage. They stare after him for a second.)

LOTTIE. Did I do something wrong?

KEVIN. No, Lottie, no. I'm sorry, Ted's just…we've had this discussion before and I guess he's feeling pressured. Not from me, of course, I'm happy with a dog.

LOTTIE. You guys have a dog?

KEVIN. No.

LOTTIE. Oh. But I thought…

KEVIN. It's just a touchy subject.

DONNA. Uh, ya think?

LOTTIE. Do you have a computer I can use?

DONNA. LOTTIE! Absolutely not!

TED. *(Re-enters, calmer.)* She can use mine. It's upstairs.

DONNA. No, she can't. Computers are very personal and people don't want you on them. Especially people that think you're a bacteria laden Petri dish.

TED. I really want to apologize about all that. I'm dealing with some big personalities at work and, you know, Lottie, you're absolutely not a buzz kill. And you can definitely use my computer. There's some Purell in the desk drawer.

DONNA. *(Stands.)* No, Lottie! We should be going!

TED. Oh, no, please don't do that. I feel like such an ass. We had Irish coffees before and now with the martinis, I don't even know what I'm saying. Look, you guys came all this way. Wouldn't you like to spend the night? We've got enough extra rooms. You can take baths. We have guest loofahs.

KEVIN. Ted, don't push them.

TED. I can make breakfast in the morning. I can make a breakfast tart!

DONNA. I knew there'd be a tart!

> *(To* **LOTTIE.***)*

> Didn't I say there'd be a tart?!

LOTTIE. You really don't want us staying here.

TED. Don't let what I said make you uncomfortable. Just because I'm dealing with some pregnant nightmares at work.

DONNA. No, you don't want us here.

TED. Why?

DONNA. Because, as she takes a deep breath, I just so happen to be one of those pregnant nightmares.

KEVIN. & TED What?

LOTTIE. *(Furious)* You're WHAT?!

KEVIN. *(Taking her martini.)* I should probably take that.

LOTTIE. You're lying!

DONNA. I think I'd know. I'm very in tune with my body. I've been throwing up like a crazy person…

LOTTIE. You're always throwing up because you're always hung-over!

DONNA. Plus I took a pregnancy test in the toilet of a Long John Silvers. Maybe the baby will be born a pirate. Little tiny hook for a hand.

LOTTIE. *(Stands up.)* You can't do this! You have to get rid of it!

DONNA. What?

LOTTIE. You have to get rid of it, mom.

DONNA. That is a moral decision that is none of your business, young lady! Besides, it's too late for that, anyway.

LOTTIE. *(To* **KEVIN** *and* **TED.***)* She's making this up! I don't know what she's after, but she's making this up!

> *(To* **DONNA.***)*

> You're crazy! You're the worst mother in the entire world and now you want to have another baby? We're essentially homeless people!

(To **KEVIN** *and* **TED**.*)*

LOTTIE. She stole this shirt from a Texaco station! She's not well!

DONNA. She's lying. She's putting on a show.

LOTTIE. It's true! You're a kleptomaniac homeless woman who smokes weed, hash when she can get it.

DONNA. Shut your mouth, Lottie.

LOTTIE. For all I know, she pimps herself out when I'm not around!

DONNA. You better shut that mouth before I shut it for you!

KEVIN. Donna!

TED. Whoa! Hey, wait a second!

LOTTIE. Now you're threatening to hit me? You know what you are? You're trash! You're stupid white trash and I wish you were dead!

(She grabs her backpack.)

KEVIN. Lottie, wait…

DONNA. Where are you going?

LOTTIE. To get you a wire hanger!

(She storms out, slamming the front door after her.)

DONNA. *(To a stunned* **KEVIN** *and* **TED**.*)* She's just tired. She's a drama queen. She'll be back…she'll be back…

(Pause.)

You know, I think maybe we will stay the night.

(Blackout.)

Scene Three

(A sink. **TED** *and* **KEVIN** *brush their teeth, apply creams, get ready for bed.)*

KEVIN. We have to disinfect the sheets after they're gone. Spray the whole room down with Lysol and Febreze.

TED. It's not like they're monkeys.

KEVIN. They're not far off. When we were in high school, Donna could pick up playing cards with her feet.

TED. You're sure we shouldn't be out looking for your niece?

KEVIN. Donna swears she does this all the time. She seems pretty sure she'll be back after she blows off some steam.

TED. I'm sure she's right.

(Pause.)

I wonder how long they'll want to stay.

KEVIN. God, you're right. We'd better get in front of that one. We don't want to have some kind of a Blanche Dubois situation. Only one night. We'll tell them only one night. I wonder what she's after.

TED. Why does she have to be after anything?

KEVIN. Please, Donna's never had a motive that wasn't ulterior. What if it's money? Ted, what if she wants to borrow money?

TED. Well, it would depend how much, I guess.

KEVIN. We can't do that. We can't loan her money. First of all, it's your money. I don't make any money.

TED. Don't do that. I hate when you do that. It's our money. It's not divided up.

KEVIN. Things are slow for you. You're trying to get your business back on track. We've got a mortgage. Maybe I should just get a job answering phones.

TED. That's not our agreement. You need time to work on your novel. And there's enough money. We've got enough money. And I don't think it would be the worst thing in the world to loan a relative some cash if they're in need.

KEVIN. Oh, no. You don't know her. It'll never stop. It'll never ever stop. She acts stupid, but underneath. I hate this. I never really wanted you to meet my family. It's not like I've lied to you, you know I'm from poor white Christmas trash, but still. You're gonna get to see it in the flesh, the genetic pool drained all over our hardwood floors. The manic episodes, the depression. I've told you it's genetic and now you're gonna have proof.

TED. So what? You get your depression from your family and your Lexapro from Duane Reade. Everything works out.

(He hugs KEVIN. KEVIN *won't let him go.)*

KEVIN. I'm gonna wear you like a coat the whole time they're here.

TED. It's gonna be fine.

KEVIN. I wish my family was more like yours. You're so lucky.

TED. All of my relatives are dead.

KEVIN. Exactly.

(Lights switch to DONNA *waiting on the couch in the dark.* LOTTIE *enters silently.)*

LOTTIE. You ruin everything. Is there anything you don't ruin?

DONNA. Thank God! I was so worried about you.

LOTTIE. You don't <u>get</u> to be worried.

DONNA. Come sit by me, come sit by mommy. I'll explain everything. I'll run my fingers through your hair. You like that. You always like that.

LOTTIE. I don't want you touching me.

DONNA. This isn't going to change anything. We can still go on that cruise ship. Maybe we'll get on one that goes to the Caribbean. I've heard that the Caribbean is beautiful.

LOTTIE. Whose baby is it?

DONNA. Or maybe we'll get on one of those Alaskan cruise lines. Check out otters and shit. You ever seen an otter? Otters are awesome. They're like little Wilford Brimleys.

LOTTIE. Whose is it?

DONNA. I can tell it's going to be a girl. My skin is already looking like shit, they steal your beauty, you know. Steal it right off your face.

LOTTIE. You know what, forget it. I don't want to talk about it anymore. We're leaving in the morning.

DONNA. You are so ungrateful, you know that? You're a hurtful ingrate.

LOTTIE. I'm an ingrate? Are you completely nuts?

DONNA. I'm sorry you don't get to live this fantasy life that you've cooked up in your head. And yes, I'm a fuck-up. I get that. But when I was growing up, I was in total hell.

LOTTIE. Yes, yes, grandma was a drunken whore. Boo hoo.

DONNA. You have no idea, Lottie. I couldn't wait to get out of that shit hole. I'm doing all of this for you. I wanted a daughter who was independent, who got out to see the world and really had a freaking interesting life, not some lame ass cul-de-sac shit. You really think that's what you want?

LOTTIE. Try me.

DONNA. Why are you so mean to me?

LOTTIE. Guess.

(*Lights switch back to* **KEVIN** *and* **TED**.)

KEVIN. (*Listening.*) That was definitely the front door. She must be back.

(*Back to* **TED**.)

I should have just hung up when I heard Donna's voice. The minute she said she was in town, I thought, "Here we go. God's gonna trouble the water."

TED. What about Lottie's dad?

KEVIN. Who the hell knows? I seriously doubt she kept in touch with him, if she even knows who he is at all. Donna's the kind of person who takes a pregnancy test in a Long John Silvers. Is it really possible for me to be related to these people?

(Pause.)

She should have had an abortion, right?

TED. Definitely.

KEVIN. I wonder if it's really too late.

(Beat.)

Oof. She brings out the worst in people, you know? If she stays more than a few days, I'll talk to her. I'll take her out to dinner and just level with her. What if she wants to stay longer than a few days?

TED. I'm sure it'll be fine. You're not…

KEVIN. What?

TED. It's almost like you're scared of her.

KEVIN. Scared? No. I'm not…she just has this way of…well, you'll see. God's gonna trouble the water.

TED. Let's tie a rope to the shore and hang on.

*(Lights switch back to **LOTTIE** and **DONNA**.)*

DONNA. I'm just trying to make a point, Lottie. I might not be a Girl Scout Troop Leader or a room mother. And magical cupcakes don't come flying out of my ass. But as far as mothers go, things could be a lot worse. Sure, I'd like it if we lived in a nice house like this, with wind chimes and fresh basil, but that's not the way it is. But you could have it a lot worse. A lot. Worse. You don't even know.

LOTTIE. Yeah, well, I think it's a little bit late in the game to ask me to start grading on a curve.

(Lights fade.)

Scene Four

*(A few months later. It's the middle of the night. The
sound of fumbling keys. Suddenly* **KEVIN** *runs in,
laughing, carrying a paper bag and drunk. He trips and
falls, hitting the floor with a thud. He starts to laugh
harder.* **DONNA** *appears, her pregnancy now starting to
show. She laughs at* **KEVIN**.*)*

DONNA. Slow down! I'm a fat monster now! You are so
wasted.

KEVIN. *(Still on the floor.)* I am not.

DONNA. Then why are you on the floor?

KEVIN. I'm resting. Don't you just love this floor? It's
all reclaimed lumber. The stain is called Black Tie
Cocktail Parquet. It sounds like our living room floor
is going to a Cotillion.

(To the floor.)

Can we come with you?

DONNA. Get up, you alcoholic.

KEVIN. I'm not an alcoholic. I'm a binge drinker. There's a
huge difference.

DONNA. Thanks for leaving me out there in the dark. I had
to grope my way to the house.

KEVIN. I was trying to get into bed before Ted wakes up.

DONNA. *(She helps him up.)* Let's put on some music.

KEVIN. No. Ted's gotta be up early tomorrow. We can't
wake them up.

DONNA. You said you wanted to talk to me over dinner
about something, then you just got pie-eyed drunk.

KEVIN. Right. That. You got any more pot?

DONNA. It's called weed now, grandpa.

*(Digs in her purse, puts various items all over the couch
and coffee table.)*

Man, I wish this thing wasn't inside me. I miss getting
stoned. This is great shit. It's got a really robust

earthy taste, with hints of blueberry. Did you taste the blueberry notes?

KEVIN. Do people really talk like that about pot?

DONNA. Weed.

(She hands him a half-smoked joint.)

KEVIN. Oh, maybe I shouldn't.

DONNA. Go ahead and toke up, I'll live vicariously.

KEVIN. It's late. If Ted wakes up, he'll wonder where I am.

DONNA. It's early. Besides, you should smoke more often. All writers get stoned and shit. It relaxes the mind. Calms the inner critic. Even Abraham Lincoln smoked the ganja.

KEVIN. You don't really think that's true, do you?

DONNA. He liked to get stoned and play the harmonica. It's true. Google it.

KEVIN. Really?

DONNA. Trust, my brother. Trust.

*(**KEVIN** tokes up. **DONNA** puts on some music.)*

KEVIN. Lower it!

DONNA. *(Lowers the music.)* You've got to get some better music. I mean, seriously. All you've got is cocktail jazz.

(Looks at the iPod.)

And it's from Pottery Barn? You get your music from a fucking couch store?

KEVIN. When are you gonna tell me what you thought about my book?

DONNA. Is that what you wanted to talk about?

KEVIN. Uh, well, it's one of the things.

DONNA. I'm gonna get some wine. I can drink <u>one</u> glass of wine. Everybody says so.

*(She disappears, **KEVIN** continues to talk.)*

KEVIN. I just wanna know what you think. I told that agent Ted got me that I'd have a full draft a couple of months ago. But the agent keeps going on about making sure

it's marketable. "Is it marketable, Kevin? We need it to
be marketable!" No wonder I can't finish it.

DONNA. *(Re-enters with wine and glasses. Pours.)* Your kitchen
is so sexy I could fuck it.

KEVIN. Don't worry about hurting my feelings. What did
you think of the book? You hate it, don't you?

DONNA. No. I mean, maybe it could use some kind of big
twist. Don't you have to have a big twist?

KEVIN. It's not that kind of book. It's Proustian and filled
with a lot of involuntary memories that maybe add up
or maybe they don't, I haven't really decided yet.

(Stops himself.)

Oh, Christ, it's just a big, heap of blather, isn't it?

DONNA. Look, we've always been honest with one another.
Honest to a fucking fault. So if you want my advice,
you should add a big twist or some vampire shit.

KEVIN. So it's not marketable?

DONNA. Don't take this the wrong way. But as far as being
marketable goes, a cookbook by Hitler would have a
better shot.

KEVIN. Oh, no. I knew it. I totally knew it.

(He takes a long drag on the joint. Exhales. **DONNA**
surreptitiously tries to inhale the smoke.)

DONNA. Don't freak out. I mean, what do I know about
fiction? Up until about four years ago, I thought the
word "misogynist" meant someone who gives massages.

KEVIN. What?

DONNA. Yeah, I know. Stupid. Lottie finally corrected me,
but only after I left a lot of people confused. "I need
to go to a misogynist. A really good one. Does anyone
know a really good misogynist?" I'm an asshole.

KEVIN. But you're right. I don't know what I'm doing
anymore. I'm just wasting my time. Mooching off of
Ted.

DONNA. Look, I've seen a lot over the last few months. And as an outside observer, I gotta tell you. You need a new direction in your life.

KEVIN. I do. I really, really do.

DONNA. You've got nothing to inspire you.

KEVIN. It's true. It's really, really true.

DONNA. You sit in this house all day long like a cat.

KEVIN. *(Sing-songy.)* I'm a cat sitting up in a house.

DONNA. Wait. Are you too stoned to follow what I'm saying? Look at me, Kevin.

KEVIN. No. I can follow you. But this weed does kind of make me feel like playing the harmonica.

DONNA. Kevin, listen to me. I've thought a lot about this and I think you and Ted should raise this baby.

KEVIN. Raise it as a what?

DONNA. As a human, you stupid pothead. You and Ted should raise this baby. You should adopt it.

KEVIN. You're funny.

DONNA. I'm dead serious.

KEVIN. *(Pause.)* Get the hell out of here.

DONNA. What?

KEVIN. *(Stands.)* Seriously, get the hell out of here. I know why you're doing this. But, you've got to go soon, Donna. I mean, you and Lottie can't stay here forever. It's been almost three months! I was supposed to tell you over dinner, but I got distracted by all the drinks you kept ordering and the joint you made me smoke.

DONNA. I'm not doing this so that we can stay here, asshole! I'm doing it because I feel sorry for you.

KEVIN. <u>You</u> feel sorry for <u>me</u>? That's hilarious.

DONNA. You wanna know why you're so blocked on your book? It's because you're afraid that if it isn't published, you're going to be forgotten. That's the problem. There's going to be no one around to remember you. Your story just ends. But when you have kids, you're immortal, Kevin. You're part of something eternal.

Without that, what have you got? It's just you and Ted growing old in this scary museum of a house and then just dying someday with nobody caring. It's the saddest story ever told.

KEVIN. It's not! It's not the saddest story ever told.

DONNA. I've known you much longer than Ted and you've always wanted to be a father. Well, technically, you always wanted to be a mother, but from the looks of things around here, we're not far off.

KEVIN. What about the baby's real father? Who is he?

DONNA. Oh, Jesus! Some Okie from Muskogee! How should I know? You know I don't believe in relationships. The point is, I'm worried about you, Kevin. You're going down a path that you never wanted to go down. Here's your chance to have your cake and eat it, too. Ted will understand. I've seen the way he looks at you. He loves you. And who knows? Maybe it'll give you something to write about. Wouldn't that be nice? And obviously it'll help me out. I mean, I can't raise another baby, look at how I fucked Lottie up six ways from Sunday. I'm in a bit of a panic here, too, you know.

KEVIN. You're talking too fast. Just stop for a second. I'm not agreeing to anything.

DONNA. I can't be in a band with a baby. I can't sing on a cruise ship. So I'm just going to have to give it away anyway. You want your unborn niece to go to strangers?

KEVIN. How is this all my fault?

DONNA. Give me your hand.

KEVIN. No.

DONNA. C'mere!

(She grabs his hand. Puts it on her stomach.)

KEVIN. Why are you?

DONNA. Shhh!

(Long pause.)

Feel that? It kicked! Did you feel that? Magic, right?

KEVIN. *(Smiles.)* Holy crap.

DONNA. She's on her way. She's on her way for you, Kevin. Talk to her.

KEVIN. I don't know what to...

(Puts his face on **DONNA***'s stomach.)*

Hey, you. Whatcha doing in there? Settle down, young lady. Don't make me stop this car!

(Jumps.)

She kicked my face!

DONNA. This is what you want, Kevin.

KEVIN. *(Stands up.)* No, no, no, no, no.

DONNA. Just think about it. Think of the kind of life you and Ted could give her.

KEVIN. Stop talking! You're confusing me! I knew some crazy shit was gonna go down when I heard you were three blocks away from us, and here you are, practically living with us, trying to get me to...oh, shit, this is so fucked up!

TED. *(Offstage.)* Kevin?

KEVIN. *(Panicked, putting out the joint.)* Shit!

DONNA. Oh, no, we woke up dad!

*(***KEVIN** *quickly waves away the smoke.* **TED** *comes downstairs in his robe.)*

Hey, Ted. Want some vino?

TED. You're drinking?

DONNA. Just a glass of wine. I can have <u>one</u> glass of wine. Everybody says so.

TED. *(Picks up the bag from the floor.)* What's this?

KEVIN. Leftovers from Shippy's. Wiener Schnitzel.

TED. Why is it on the floor?

KEVIN. Sorry. The Wiener Schnitzel is really great, but the restaurant is kind of a shit hole.

DONNA. Shippy's isn't a shit hole. It's fifteen different kinds of awesome.

KEVIN. I wish you would have come with us.

TED. *(Aside, to* KEVIN.*)* Did you talk to her?

KEVIN. Working on it.

    (Embraces TED.*)*

    D'ya miss me?

TED. Um, sure. Are you drunk? Is he drunk?

KEVIN. I'm just tipsy.

DONNA. And stoned.

KEVIN. Oh my God, she is such a liar!

TED. It's almost two in the morning. What did you two do at Shippy's?

DONNA. We gave ourselves Native American names.

KEVIN. *(Laughing.)* She's Moose With Papoose.

DONNA. And he's Squatsoncox!

    (They crack up.)

    And then we dined and dashed!

TED. Are you crazy? Why would you do that? People know us around here.

KEVIN. It was kind of funny.

    *(*TED *glares at him.* KEVIN *turns on* DONNA.*)*

    It was a terrible thing to do.

TED. You're going back there tomorrow and apologizing. And paying them back. And leaving an extra big tip.

DONNA. Jeeze, Ted, remember when you used to be fun?

TED. And can you turn that music off? You're gonna wake up Lottie.

    *(*KEVIN *stumbles over to the iPod dock and accidentally turns the music up.)*

    Turn it down! Down!

    *(*KEVIN *quickly turns it down.)*

KEVIN. Sorry, sorry! Everything looks kinda pixilated.

DONNA. He's not gonna throw up, is he?

KEVIN. Blech. Why did you plant that seed in my mind?

TED. We don't throw up in living rooms, Kevin. Kevin?! We do not throw up on new hardwood flooring!

LOTTIE. *(Offstage.)* Mom?

TED. Oh, great. Now Lottie's up.

> (**LOTTIE** *comes down the stairs wearing an oversized "Hooters" T-Shirt.*)

LOTTIE. What's going on?

DONNA. It's a party, biotch! Come get on the party bus! Lottie can do that robot dance. Do that robot dance, Lottie!

TED. Sorry, Lottie.

KEVIN. I'm definitely going to puke.

LOTTIE. *(To* **TED**.*)* Go hold him over the toilet. And see if you have any Gatorade. You're gonna wanna keep him hydrated and make sure he has enough electrolytes.

TED. Shouldn't I give him coffee?

LOTTIE. It'll dehydrate him.

KEVIN. Oh, God.

LOTTIE. Go.

TED. Thanks. Come on, you.

> (**TED** *helps a moaning* **KEVIN** *off.* **LOTTIE** *turns off the music and takes* **DONNA***'s glass of wine away from her.*

LOTTIE. Why do you keep ruining things? From now on, you're grounded from ruining things.

DONNA. I know what I'm doing.

LOTTIE. Every day that goes by, they hate us more. You should be focusing on what we're going to do next. That's what you should be focusing on.

DONNA. You don't know all the tricks mommy has up her sleeve.

TED. *(Re-enters.)* We don't have any Gatorade.

LOTTIE. Juice is better than nothing.

DONNA. Isn't my little girl smart?

TED. Where'd you learn all this?

LOTTIE. Van school.

> (*TED exits.*)

We're gonna have another mouth to feed soon, so we need to figure out what we're going to do.

> (*Starts collecting* DONNA*'s junk and putting it back in her purse.*)

And we are guests here, so you might want to control your suburban sprawl!

TED. (*Re-enters.*) He's just gonna sleep on the bathroom floor for now. I put him on top of a towel.

LOTTIE. On his side, so he can't choke.

TED. Right. Is that what you're using for pajamas these days?

LOTTIE. (*Looks at her shirt.*) My PJ's were falling apart, so this is what I sleep in now.

TED. Jesus, we're going shopping tomorrow.

> (*He exits.*)

DONNA. What about me? Why don't I get to go shopping?

LOTTIE. Because you're grounded. Now go to sleep!

> (LOTTIE *turns out the lights and heads off.* DONNA *goes to the doorway and calls off gently.*)

DONNA. Kevin…this baby is coming just for you, bro. Just for you.

> (*The sound of* KEVIN *throwing in the other room.* DONNA *finds her glass of wine and downs it. Blackout.*)

Scene Five

(Lights up on **LOTTIE** *and* **TED** *at a table in a mall, eating fast food. Several shopping bags around them.)*

TED. *(Puts down fries.)* Why am I eating these fries? And I asked her not to put mayonnaise on this sandwich.

LOTTIE. Why do you care? You're not fat. You don't have to watch what you eat.

TED. I'm a gay man. It's part of the gig.

(Scrapes mayonnaise off the bun.)

When you're as old as me, you'll see. Your metabolism will change and the party will be over.

*(***LOTTIE*** thinks for a second. Scrapes the mayonnaise off her bun, too.)*

Oh, hey, don't do that. You're too young to worry about that.

LOTTIE. Thanks for the clothes.

TED. Oh, no big deal. We should hit a few shops in town. This place is kind of tragic, really. Just a tragic outlet mall. With fast food workers who want to make me fat with all their mayonnaise.

LOTTIE. I kind of love it here…

TED. Yeah, okay. I do, too. They've got a Barneys and a Saks, for Christ's sake.

(Pause.)

Thanks for your help last night. I don't know what's gotten into Kevin.

LOTTIE. Did you take me shopping because you want to ask how to get rid of mom and me?

TED. What? No! Of course not.

LOTTIE. So you just didn't like my "Hooters" nightgown? There's no other reason?

TED. None. Well, one, maybe. Look, hey, it's none of my business, but the kind of life you and your mom lead.

It can't be good for you. I mean, do you have any friends your own age?

LOTTIE. We move around a lot. So I'm never at one school long enough to become anything more than the semi-homeless freak. Then it's back on the road. Just me and the crazy lady.

TED. How is that right, Lottie? You should be around people your own age. In a house. On a street. In a community. On a cheerleading team.

LOTTIE. On a cheerleading team? Barf.

TED. Okay, maybe that's my personal fantasy. But the point is, this kind of existence isn't right.

LOTTIE. I keep thinking, if I could just track down my dad. Last I heard he was in Champagne-Urbana.

TED. Champagne-Urbana. That always sounds like a made up place to me.

LOTTIE. It's a total misnomer, too. Because it's not urban and there's very little champagne.

TED. How've you been trying to get a hold of him?

LOTTIE. Mom is totally evasive about him. I asked her one time to just tell me what he looked like. And she said, "I don't know. Kinda like Mr. Peanut, only less fancy." I assume that means he's probably bald and wears a monocle. That's about all I've got to go on. That and some now defunct email. I did a search on the Internet and there are a couple of websites that help you find people, but you have to have a credit card.

TED. Well, that's easy. I'll pay for it.

LOTTIE. Really?

TED. Really. Just give me his name and any info you've got.

LOTTIE. If you can get me his number, I promise I'll get us out of your house. I don't care what it takes. I know how to manipulate mom.

TED. It's not that I want you out. I like you, Lottie. It's just, with your mother around… Kevin's always been very… what's the word?

LOTTIE. Impressionable?

TED. Exactly. He was so adrift when I first met him. He wanted so desperately to be a writer. And I knew I could help him out. A few years after we met, he actually got published in the New Yorker.

LOTTIE. Whoa? Uncle Kevin?

TED. Right? Impressive huh?

LOTTIE. Like a short story? That's amazing.

TED. Well, it wasn't really a short story so much as a…

LOTTIE. Non-fiction piece?

TED. It was…it was actually a cartoon. A cartoon contest. Where you come up with a caption for a cartoon.

LOTTIE. Oh.

TED. But they put his name in the magazine. So technically he was published in The New Yorker. And just because he's never published any actual fiction doesn't mean he lacks talent.

LOTTIE. Of course not.

TED. I just wish he would finish this book, you know? I think it would be a real watershed moment for him. Then his agent can send it out and in the meantime, maybe he could get a part-time job or something. A little extra cash wouldn't hurt. The bigger design firms have been killing me lately.

LOTTIE. Oh, no. Then we shouldn't have…

(She points to the shopping bags.)

TED. Oh, no! No! Times aren't that tough! I just need him to accomplish something. For both of our sakes. And with your mother here, the wheels are starting to come of the cart and…

(Pauses.)

Oh, you know, we shouldn't be talking about this. Let's not say I said anything.

LOTTIE. Don't worry. I won't say a word. I'm a bank safe.

(Lights switch back to the living room. **KEVIN** *slowly walks into the living room, looking like hell. He sees a bottle of Gatorade on the coffee table with a note on it. He reads the note.)*

KEVIN. Drink me.

*(***KEVIN** *shrugs. Takes a swig. Slowly sits down.* **DONNA** *enters, also looking like a wreck.)*

You look like Shelley Winters in "The Poseidon Adventure". Did you even look at yourself in the mirror before you came downstairs?

DONNA. Pffft. I figure there's nobody but us girls, so why bother?

KEVIN. Way to slack. You smell a little gamey, you know.

DONNA. You're not exactly camera ready, yourself.

(Notices a note, reads it.)

Dear mom, your prenatal pills are on the kitchen counter. Don't take them with beer. I made sandwiches for you and Uncle Kevin. Please don't bother him while he's working.

(Puts down the note.)

Is that kid awesome or what?

KEVIN. How much did you drink last night?

DONNA. Oh, for Christ's sake. Mom drank when she was pregnant with us and look how we turned out!

KEVIN. Case rested.

(Pause.)

You were saying some pretty crazy stuff last night.

DONNA. Kevin. I meant every word.

KEVIN. That's not funny. Besides, I'm too hung over to have this discussion anyway. I'm supposed to be working now. Didn't Lottie say not to bother me while I'm working?

DONNA. Fine. Work!

KEVIN. I will!

DONNA. Then do!

(**KEVIN** *opens up his laptop and stares at it.* **DONNA** *sits stewing for a moment, then jumps up off the couch.*)

You know what? Screw this!

KEVIN. What?

(**DONNA** *storms off.* **KEVIN** *shakes his head, goes back to his laptop, a couple of backpacks come flying onstage.* **DONNA** *enters, kicking them to the couch, her arms full of laundry.*)

What are you doing?

DONNA. *(Packing furiously.)* Lottie and I are so out of here! I offer you a fucking part of myself and all I get is this shit storm in return! You think I can't find other people that'll take this baby? That would kill for this baby? This was your one chance and you're such a Goddamn pussy that you fucked it up!

KEVIN. Okay, you're not being rational.

DONNA. I'm not being rational? I'm not being rational? You're the one who's not being rational! You think chances like this are gonna come along every fucking day of the week?

KEVIN. You know how Ted feels about this…

DONNA. What about what you want, Kevin?

KEVIN. I want what Ted wants, we want the same things! That's how things work in a relationship.

DONNA. "That's how things work in a relationship" Jesus Christ, I can't fucking wait for the day your testicles descend.

KEVIN. You know what? Go! Get the hell out!

DONNA. Oh, I am! I'm getting the rest of my shit and then, poof! I'm a magic trick! I'm gone!

(**DONNA** *storms off. Lights switch.*)

TED. *(Picking at his fries again.)* Damn it! I'm eating these damn fries again! Take them away from me.

LOTTIE. I'm the teenage girl, here. I'm the one that's supposed to have body issues.

TED. Well, you know, deep down we're all just a bunch of teenage girls. The whole world.

(Pause.)

Except maybe you. How old are you again?

LOTTIE. I just turned fifteen in May.

TED. Did you do anything special?

LOTTIE. Mom got me a couple of lottery tickets and a Little Debbie snack cake with a candle in it.

TED. Jesus.

LOTTIE. I know. Talk about Dickensian.

TED. Look, you can't go on like this. And we can't just assume that your father is going to step up to the plate. I'm thinking, I'm thinking I should just call child services. I mean, this is crazy.

LOTTIE. You can't do that! We're trusting you! You can't call child services on mom, what'll happen to me? I don't want to live in some foster home. Have you seen the people that take in foster children? They're always obese. Morbidly obese! They're the kind of people that just want the money from the state so they can order in Pizza Hut until Richard Simmons shows up with a bouquet of balloons! They're the kind of people that can't get out of the house unless you take down a wall with a chainsaw!

TED. You've got a very active imagination, Lottie. But you can't go on like this.

LOTTIE. I just have a few more years to go. Two and a half more years and I'll be an adult. You can't turn me in. I know mom's screwed up, but I can't live with strangers. Morbidly obese strangers. Think of the smell!

TED. Look, I just feel really stuck about all this.

LOTTIE. *(Breaking down.)* Please don't call anyone. Please.

TED. Oh, boy. Don't get upset. Please, Lottie. Do you want a McFlurry?

(She shakes her head.)

You know what we're gonna do? We're gonna throw you a birthday party. How's that? Would that make you feel better?

LOTTIE. I don't need your pity birthday party.

TED. Well, you're getting it. We'll invite people.

LOTTIE. I don't know any people.

TED. That's your problem! You need to be around people your own age.

LOTTIE. No, I can't do that. Please.

TED. We'll go right now and introduce you to Anne and Vivian's kids. They've got a girl your age. Trina. She can take you around town and introduce you. You've been living with adults too long.

LOTTIE. Please, I don't…people don't like me. They think I'm weird. I am weird, compared to them.

TED. Let's just stop by Anne and Vivian's. It's a start. And you're gonna have that birthday party whether you like it or not.

LOTTIE. But…

TED. But what?

LOTTIE. Well…

(Smiles to herself.)

I would kind of like an iPod.

*(Lights switch back to the living room. **KEVIN** sits on the couch, deep in thought. **DONNA** enters with more bags.)*

KEVIN. Donna?

DONNA. No, it's all good. I'm going. I'm gone. I'm gonna go pick up Lottie at that mall and then it's gonna be like the ground opened up and swallowed us. You'll never see us again. But get this, bro. This is your last chance. I walk out that door and it's over. So you make your decision. Is this it? Is it over? Am I going?

(Pause.)

Am I going, Kevin?

KEVIN. I don't know.

DONNA. What?

KEVIN. I don't know.

DONNA. Look at your face. You can't lie anymore, Kevin. You wanna be a mommy.

KEVIN. Donna?

DONNA. Yeah?

KEVIN. I wanna be a mommy.

(Blackout.)

End of Act One

ACT TWO

Scene One

(Lights come up on the living room. There are birthday streamers and balloons. **DONNA**, *wearing a birthday hat, sits scowling on the couch. She picks up a bound photo album and leafs through it.* **TED** *enters with flowers and party hats.)*

DONNA. Who put this together?

TED. Kevin and I enjoy scrap booking.

DONNA. Why, sucking dick doesn't make you feel gay enough?

TED. *(Ignoring her.)* You know, you could help if you felt like it.

DONNA. I don't. *(Turns a page.)* I can't believe I never noticed these. Jesus, is that what Christmas looks like around here? All these bows and wreaths. A gingerbread house with stained glass windows?

TED. You make them out of melted Jolly Ranchers.

DONNA. What do you do on the actual day?

TED. Christmas? Oh, exchange gifts. Maybe go out to dinner or see a movie.

DONNA. A movie? You work yourselves up into this decorating frenzy, this homosexual orgy of excess and then when the actual day comes, you go see a movie? That's just depressing.

TED. It's not. It's fine.

DONNA. Sure would be a great place to grow up.

TED. *(Stops what he's doing.)* Why would you bring that up? I mean, seriously, why?

DONNA. *(Picks up another album.)* Sorry. I'm in a mood.

(Opens the album.)

What the hell is this? Kevin said we weren't invited to your wedding because it wasn't a big deal. There are like five hundred people in this picture! And who are those guys? Are those footmen?

TED. They're called cater-waiters, not footmen. We don't live in a Disney animated feature, Donna.

DONNA. Could have fooled me.

LOTTIE. *(Offstage.)* Can I come in yet?

TED. Absolutely not!

LOTTIE. *(Offstage.)* Ha! I hate you!

DONNA. *(Closes the album.)* I'm sure we were super busy that day, anyway.

TED. Speaking of being busy, whatever happened to that audition? The cruise ship thing?

DONNA. My friend's still trying to work it out. It's not all black and white. That's the thing about a career in the arts.

TED. I'm not sure which word is funnier. "Career" or "arts".

(KEVIN enters, carries a large box.)

KEVIN. Sorry I'm late. The cake is gorgeous.

TED. What took you so long?

KEVIN. The two Bobs had an emergency. I had to watch the twins for a few minutes.

TED. You were babysitting the twins?

KEVIN. For like five minutes.

TED. Did you know what to do?

KEVIN. I was babysitting, not handling snakes. Wanna see the cake?

(He opens the box and stares at it.)

DONNA. You guys, this is all too much. I mean, this thing looks like a wedding cake. Does everything have to be so over the top with you homos?

TED. Pretty much. Let's see.

(KEVIN takes the cake out of the box. It is, in fact, elaborate.)

Jesus, that is pretty spectacular.

KEVIN. It looks like a Victorian hat.

DONNA. "It looks like a Victorian hat!" Christ, Kev, you make Charles Nelson Reilly sound like the Marlboro Man.

TED. What's her problem?

DONNA. When Kevin and I were growing up, we would have killed to get a cake like that. We would have killed to get any kind of cake.

LOTTIE. *(Offstage.)* Is Uncle Kevin back? Can I come in yet? I wanna come in!

TED. Not yet!

(Takes the cake.)

I'll go put candles in it. Though it seems stupid to put candles in such a pretty cake, but you've gotta have candles on your birthday, right?

DONNA. It's not her birthday.

TED. You know what I mean.

(He's gone.)

DONNA. Why haven't you talked to him yet? Look how geeked out he is over Lottie's non-birthday. Just think if it was his own kid.

KEVIN. I don't know. He's gonna freak out.

DONNA. Don't be such a bottom. I'm sick of your baby ways! You have to talk to him. He might change his mind if you put it the right way. Besides, why does he get the final say? Don't you get a fifty percent vote?

KEVIN. Just let me handle this, okay?

DONNA. I'm just getting antsy, man. Time is ticking. I gotta know what we're doing here.

KEVIN. I don't know. This is all happening so fast.

DONNA. You're fucking backing out on me? You can't do that. We had a deal. We had a fucking arrangement!

KEVIN. Shh! Jesus, Donna! Okay, shhh! Right now you're at about a nine and a half and I'm gonna need you to dial it down to like a four or a five.

DONNA. *(Sighs.)* Whatever. This should be a baby shower, that's what this should be.

KEVIN. Just don't bring up the other day. It's not your place.

DONNA. You know, a few years ago, when I told Lottie about you and Ted being together, she asked me, "Which one's the woman?" And I was like, "It doesn't work that way." But now I know I was wrong. There is a woman in your relationship, Kevin. And it's you. And take it from someone who knows. It sucks to be the woman. Don't be the woman.

KEVIN. *(Putting on a birthday tiara.)* I am not the woman!

DONNA. Well, you're certainly not the man, bro. You're certainly not the man.

KEVIN. Shut up.

(TED *comes back in with the cake. They immediately shut up.)*

Oh, hey, can I call her?

(TED *nods.)*

Hey, Lottie come on down!

(LOTTIE *enters. Stares at the cake.)*

LOTTIE. Oh my God! It's so awesome!

DONNA. Awesomely gay.

LOTTIE. Is Trina coming?

TED. Oh, sorry. Vivian said she had a riding lesson.

LOTTIE. She and her friends thought I was a freak, right? I told you I suck around people my age. I should have never tried to explain malapropisms to them.

TED. Don't be crazy. Trina had a riding lesson.

KEVIN. Okay, make a wish!

(Starts to sing with **TED.***)*

KEVIN. AND TED Happy Birth-

*(***LOTTIE** *blows the candles out.)*

KEVIN. Whoa, Lottie! You're supposed to wait until we finish singing.

LOTTIE. Sorry. I just got a little excited.

TED. It happens.

LOTTIE. Let's not eat it yet. I want to look at it some more.

DONNA. I'm starving! Don't be a dick, Lottie, cut the cake.

TED. It's her cake, we don't have to eat it right now if she doesn't want us to.

DONNA. You know, this is the problem with America. Parents let kids make all the decisions. They get to call all the shots. When I was growing up, we did what the adults wanted to do. We didn't have all this control, get all these choices. If we were done eating in a restaurant, we had to sit quietly while mommy and daddy finished their coffee. If we were going on a car trip, we had to have an imagination, not a DVD of "Dora-Square-Pants-Whoever-the-Fuck!" And we used to have to earn things as a kid. Now, everybody on the swim team gets a trophy, no matter if they win or lose. Nobody's allowed to learn what it's like to fail, because God forbid they aren't told what a winner they are every five seconds.

TED. What is your problem?

DONNA. I'm pregnant and I want some cake!

LOTTIE. You know what, just give her some cake.

TED. No.

DONNA. You said it's Lottie's cake. And she said I can have some. Who are you? The one who makes the decisions? The decider? You're the George Bush of everyone's cake allotment?

TED. *(To* KEVIN.*)* Um, a little help here?

KEVIN. Donna, you're being a hormonal bitch. Eat an apple.

LOTTIE. I really don't care. Give her whatever it takes to shut her up.

DONNA. No. I don't want any cake now. I'm not gonna eat any of your precious cake, so suck it.

LOTTIE. Why are you being like this?

DONNA. Because where's my party? You guys missed my birthday several years in a row and nobody's buying me a cake or school clothes or an iPod.

LOTTIE. You got me an iPod?

TED. Way to ruin a surprise, Donna.

DONNA. You know, if this kind of gross, over the top, spoiling is the way you guys think you're supposed to raise kids, I might just reconsider giving you my baby after all.

TED. What?

KEVIN. Donna, I swear to God…

TED. What is she talking about?

DONNA. Oh, please, Kevin. Grow a pair!

(*To* TED.)

Kevin and I talked and we think it's best that you two adopt this baby. It's what Kevin wants. It's a win-win. Well, there are three of us, so it's a win-win-win.

LOTTIE. You're joking, right?

DONNA. It's what Kevin wants. We talked about it.

TED. Oh, you and Kevin talked about it. Oh, I see. I see, that's fine, then.

KEVIN. Can we not do this now? It's Lottie's birthday.

DONNA. It's not her birthday!

TED. She is kidding, right? I mean, she's joking.

KEVIN. I think this is something we should discuss calmly and alone and at a time that is not right now.

TED. You're right. This is a totally insane topic that we should put a pin in.

DONNA. What?

TED. Let's make this whole conversation a parking lot item, okay?

DONNA. A parking lot item? Who says that?

TED. Who says that? I'll tell you who says that. Business people. People who do business. It's a short hand used by people who actually trade their skills and/ or wares for actual money. And pay taxes. And FICA. Responsible business people who do responsible business things in exchange for currency. Dollars. Sometimes maybe even a few British pounds. Or Euros, if their skills or wares are of an international flare. That's who talks like that.

DONNA. *(To* **KEVIN***)* Is that directed at me or you?

KEVIN. Lottie, why don't you open up your iPod.

LOTTIE. Well, now that I know what it is…

KEVIN. *(Shouts)* Open up your iPod and act surprised!

LOTTIE. *(Opens it in silence, weakly feigns surprise.)* Wow, an iPod! Yay.

KEVIN. There are more presents to open.

LOTTIE. *(To* **DONNA.***)* What did you give me?

DONNA. I gave you life, okay?

LOTTIE. Is that what they call it?

DONNA. Hardy-har.

KEVIN. *(Hands* **LOTTIE** *another gift.)* Open this. It's a sweater. Damn it, why do we keep doing that?!

TED. Was this the plan all along? You get knocked up and try and pawn off the baby on the two homos?

LOTTIE. She doesn't have those kinds of planning skills, trust me.

(To **DONNA**.*)*

You don't, right? Because this is the stupidest thing
you've ever tried.

TED. And something tells me you've got a list of stupid
things that's longer than the Old and New Testaments
combined.

DONNA. Can I have some wine? I can have <u>one</u> glass of
wine. Everybody says so.

TED. And what do you get in return, Donna? Let's say
you've brainwashed Kevin into actually wanting this
thing. I'm sure there's some price tag attached, right?

DONNA. Oh, screw you.

KEVIN. Parking lot!

DONNA. You know what your problem is, Ted?

KEVIN. Parking lot! Parking lot! Parking lot!!

TED. *(Calmly.)* No, you're right. You're right. Go ahead,
Lottie.

LOTTIE. *(Pulls a sweater out of the box.)* Hey, look, a sweater.

TED. And another thing I don't get. Another thing that just
blows my mind…

(Slaps down another present.)

Barnes and Noble gift card.

(To **KEVIN**.*)*

…is how you could agree to this, to something that I
don't want in the slightest, without even talking to me.

KEVIN. I didn't agree to anything.

DONNA. Well, that's just a flat out lie.

LOTTIE. *(Opens the gift certificate box.)* A gift card! Think of
all the books I can buy! I love books!

KEVIN. Everyone please shut up and let's eat some
Goddamn cake!

DONNA. I thought we couldn't cut it.

LOTTIE. Oh my God, we can cut it! We can cut the cake!
Look, I'm cutting it, alright? I'm cutting it!

(She starts cutting like crazy. Tossing pieces on plates.)

Everybody take a piece. Everybody just eat the fancy cake and enjoy my non-birthday un-celebration and shut up.

(Everyone eats in silence.)

KEVIN. It's good cake.

*(***TED*** *slams down his cake and starts to go.)*

Where are you going?

TED. I'm going to get some ice cream. Because you know I can't eat cake without ice cream.

DONNA. *(Mumbling to herself.)* You should have gotten an ice cream cake then. Why didn't you think of that? You thought of everything else. Ice cream cake would have killed two birds with one stone.

TED. Also, if I stay here any longer, I might have to murder everyone. Not you, Lottie, it's your special day. But everyone else. So I'm going to drive out to Carvel and have some private ice cream time.

(Starts to go, stops, pulls an envelope out of his pocket and hands it to ***LOTTIE.****)*

I almost forgot. One more present.

LOTTIE. Aren't you just going to tell me what it is?

TED. Don't you want to be surprised?

LOTTIE. I don't know, it kind of feels like we set up a little tradition here.

TED. It's your dad's phone number and address. If he still lives in Champagne-Urbana, that is.

(He exits. ***LOTTIE*** *tears the envelope open.)*

LOTTIE. Oh my God.

DONNA. Lottie, give me that. Give me that.

KEVIN. *(Grabs his coat, heads for the door.)* Ted, wait up! Ted!

(To ***DONNA.****)*

You're blocking my car! I'm gonna take your van!

DONNA. Fine, go!

(**KEVIN** *exits.* **DONNA** *lunges for the letter.*)

DONNA. Lottie, give that to me!

(**LOTTIE** *puts the letter behind her back.*)

Lottie!

LOTTIE. No! I'm calling him!

DONNA. He's an asshole, Lottie.

LOTTIE. So? Every guy you've ever dated is an asshole. I've seen so many assholes, I could be a proctologist.

DONNA. Don't…please…

LOTTIE. I'm calling him. I'm more of an adult than you will ever be and I've made an adult decision and I am calling him.

DONNA. Okay. Okay.

(*She sighs, sits down.*)

Suit yourself.

LOTTIE. Leave.

DONNA. You don't want me here?

LOTTIE. I don't want you anywhere.

DONNA. You might need me for backup. In case he doesn't remember.

(**LOTTIE** *hesitates.*)

You wanna call or you wanna argue?

LOTTIE. Just don't say anything!

(**LOTTIE** *dials the phone.*)

Hello? Hi…is this, I'm looking for James Freeman. Jim Freeman. I'm…no I'm not selling anything. No, I… well, this is awkward, but you used to know my mom. Donna Adams? No, she said you worked together at a nightclub in Champagne-Urbana. In the late nineties… this ringing a bell? Ha. No, her name is Donna. Donna Adams. She worked with you behind the bar?

(**DONNA** *points at her ass.*)

LOTTIE. She…um, there's a tattoo of the Playboy bunny
    on her right ass cheek. I thought that might jog your
    memory. Yeah. Yep. That's her. Anyway, this is really
    strange, but she said that you, you know, hooked up.
    Yes, you did. I know you did. No, you did. Because
    you're, Jim, you're my dad so…that's a lot of proof.
    Hello? Hello? Are you there? Look I don't want
    anything from you, I just wanted to hear your voice, I
    don't want money or anything. I'd sent you a couple of
    emails, but they all came back and so…well, of course
    she's sure it was you. I don't care how many guys she
    slept with, she knows it was you. I'm not going to keep
    calling you or upset your life or anything, it's just that
    I wanted to talk to you or maybe, could you send me
    a picture? No, this isn't a joke. What? No, please, I
    just wanted to…okay. Okay. No, I won't call you again.
    Okay. I'm sorry. I said I was sorry. Right. Okay. Bye.

(She hangs up the phone. She starts to cry. **DONNA** *goes
to her and starts to put her arm around her.)*

Get off of me.

(Lights fade.)

Scene Two

(A bench. **TED** *sits eating an ice cream cone. The sound of a van pulling up.* **KEVIN** *quietly approaches. He sits next to* **TED**.*)*

TED. You took their van?

KEVIN. Uh-huh.

TED. Does it smell like tacos in there? Because I always imagined it would smell like tacos.

KEVIN. It's more like foot. Feet. Many, many feet. Like if a caterpillar was the size of a horse and wore shoes for a year and then put all of those shoes inside Donna's van, that's what it kind of smells like.

*(***TED** *offers him a lick of his ice cream cone.)*

No thanks.

(Pause.)

So, you're mad.

TED. I don't know if I'm mad, really. I'm just really confused. But I thought we weren't going to talk about this now. I thought this was a parking lot item.

KEVIN. Well, look around. We're actually in a parking lot.

TED. *(Looks around.)*

Shit. You're right. It's a little one, but I guess technically it is a parking lot.

(Sighs.)

You don't really want this, Kevin. I know that deep down, she's just, I don't know, put some kind of voodoo spell on you. She's a grifter. No, she's a barnacle. We just need to scrape her off the side of the boat and everything will get back to normal.

KEVIN. Okay, great, but you don't think we could use, I don't know, a little change?

TED. A little change? A little change is something you put in a soda machine. This would totally obliterate life as we know it.

KEVIN. So you don't think we're missing out on something?

TED. Missing out on what? Look at what your sister has done to Lottie.

KEVIN. But we're not like Donna! Jesus! You think we're like Donna? Donna's a certified cuckoo clock. We're Ted and Kevin. Kevin and Ted. We live in a fancy restored house and know how to wash and match our clothing. You make couscous. I was published in "The New Yorker". Sort of. We both know what the word "misogynist" means. My God, how can you put us on the level of Donna?

TED. Just stop, okay? Just stop for a second and tell me why now, all the sudden, you've magically acquired the need to parent an infant. I mean, let's be real. Our hatred of children is one of the things that brought us together.

KEVIN. Our hatred of other people's children. It might be different with our own. I'm sure plenty of parents love their own kids, but still hate everybody else's. And God, we could teach those entitled parents running around town how it's done. We'd be an example.

TED. We'd be a cautionary tale.

KEVIN. You don't really think that.

TED. And this is what you do, this is what you've always done. You think you want something, but you haven't thought it all the way through.

KEVIN. Don't patronize me. Really, I hate it when you do that. I'm not an idiot. I know it would be a ton of work, but, hey, I'm sorry, I guess she kind of woke something up in me. Ever since they've been here, our lives have seemed so incredibly small. What's going to happen to us as we get older?

TED. We're going to have a great time. We'll travel, we'll learn to speak Italian. I'll have more time to cook, you can write. That's the future we always planned. It's an amazingly great future. People dream of having that future, Kevin.

KEVIN. I guess it just suddenly seems kind of lonely.

TED. Lonely? I don't feel lonely. I'm with you. Are you saying you feel lonely when it's just the two of us?

KEVIN. No. Well, maybe. A little. And I just got excited, maybe over excited, at the idea of what a good father you'd be.

TED. Don't make this into some kind of compliment that I've misunderstood.

KEVIN. No. No, it's just with everything you've done for Lottie. I guess I just thought that someday, maybe…

(Pause.)

I mean, all the joking and ranting aside, are you sure there isn't a little tiny part of you that wants to have a kid.

TED. Jesus, Kevin, I already have a kid!

KEVIN. What?

TED. Look, I love you, Kevin. But for all intents and purposes you are not an adult. I know, mathematically you are. Physically? Obviously. But emotionally?

KEVIN. Emotionally what?

TED. Never mind.

KEVIN. Oh, no. No, no, no. I'm an emotional eight year old.

TED. Not eight. Maybe fourteen.

KEVIN. Oh, well, that's an improvement.

TED. Oh, come on, Kevin. You have to be coddled and supported financially, not that I have ever balked at that, not that I didn't suggest it even, but you have to be taken care of. You're needy and dependent and maybe that's what I love about you, because I like to be the one taking care of people. But I get to choose the people, Kevin. Get it? I get to choose the people and I already have my plate full.

KEVIN. Wow.

TED. I'm sorry. Maybe that's not the way it should have come out. But, let's be practical here. Let's just take the financial aspect of this little thing you've agreed to behind my back. I just lost two bids last week. I have frighteningly little income. I had to lay off half of my staff and we still have to pay the mortgage and the electric bill and whatever the hell else we need and now you want to take in a baby and pay for clothes and school and college and whatnot when you aren't even bringing in one red cent.

KEVIN. Christ, I had no idea that you resented me so much. This is good. This is illuminating. Who knew there was so much hiding out in the parking lot?

TED. I don't resent you!

KEVIN. You just think I'm incompetent.

TED. I just believe that the past predicts the future. Okay?

KEVIN. Stop talking corporate-speak!

TED. All I'm saying is, you've never been the kind of guy who could take care of things.

KEVIN. Examples! Give me some examples.

TED. No, no, no. Come on, this isn't us.

KEVIN. You come on, examples! Support your thesis.

TED. Let's just stop.

KEVIN. No, you can't just say I'm this complete failure, this train wreck…you know, fuck you! If you can't come up with something, then you're just being an asshole!

TED. The book.

KEVIN. What?

TED. I don't know, it's been ten years and if you were a writer you would, hmmm, let's see, I don't know, maybe write something? Or if not, then realize that that dog won't hunt and take some initiative and temp or learn a trade that you can actually perform.

(**KEVIN**, *hurt and stunned, stares at* **TED**. **TED** *relents.*)

Wait, I didn't mean to say that like that. I'm just, I'm just…I'm just trying to…to…to open the kimono on this one.

KEVIN. Open the kimono?

TED. Yeah. It's a...

(*Sighs.*)

It's a business term.

KEVIN. It's also confusing and probably racist.

TED. It means I'm just trying to be honest with you, to lay our cards on the table. I am not raising a baby. That's not anything that I want to pursue. So, I don't know what to tell you.

KEVIN. So if this is something I want to pursue, then we're done? Ten years and we're done?

TED. I don't know. I...I guess so.

KEVIN. Wow. That is one very open kimono.

(*Pause*)

So, I guess we're screwed then.

TED. No we're not. Don't say that.

KEVIN. But we are.

TED. Why? Why do you say that?

KEVIN. Because that's what we are.

(*Lights switch.*)

Scene Three

(Late at night. DONNA, *in her robe, picks at a piece of cake.* KEVIN *slowly enters, still wearing his coat. He's drunk.)*

DONNA. What's going on? Did you and Ted hash things out? He came home earlier, but I didn't want to talk to him until I knew what was what. You know me, I hate to rock the boat.

KEVIN. Did you know that Shippy's real name is Shippy's Pumpernickel Restaurant?

DONNA. You're wasted. You didn't drive all the way here by yourself, did you?

KEVIN. Don't worry, your van is still a van. I met so many awesome new people. Real people. You know, like us.

DONNA. Sit down. You should drink some water.

KEVIN. I already drank some stuff. Some Hefeweizen, though I don't like beer, it was very good. And Shippy, who is super cool, gave me some gratis goulash. That's not the name of it, it was just called goulash, but it happened to be gratis. Ergo, I put the two words together. Because that's what I do. I'm a writer. A putter together of words. They were funny people…I got…I…got…

(Pulls out a napkin.)

Some good ideas for a book. Or short story…or something. Which, according to Ted, I will probably never finish.

DONNA. What happened with Ted?

KEVIN. Oh, just Armageddon, that's all.

DONNA. Sit down. I have to know what we're doing here. You're freaking me out.

KEVIN. Ten years and he thinks I'm a fucking loser. Unable to finish anything. Irresponsible. And he's right. He opened up his kimono and the truth fell right out onto the parking lot.

DONNA. What?

KEVIN. It's over.

DONNA. Look, babies bring people together. I've seen it happen all the time.

(Touches her stomach.)

This is the glue you two need.

KEVIN. Well, Ted doesn't want your glue, Donna.

DONNA. You can't do this to me! You got into a fight. Big fucking deal. Listen, you guys have got to take this baby.

KEVIN. I thought there were a million people who would kill to have it.

DONNA. I can't do that. All that shit I said before, that was just to scare you. Do you think I'm really the kind of person who could give my baby away to strangers? If that were true, Lottie'd be living in some lame ass suburb sipping on a juice box! So you gotta take this baby, I can't do it all alone.

KEVIN. You won't be alone.

DONNA. What?

KEVIN. I'm coming with you.

DONNA. No you're not.

KEVIN. I'm going to prove to everybody that I am not a mooch or a child or that I've allowed myself to be infant...infanta-cised? Lized? Infantilized? Is that a word?

DONNA. Fuck if I know!

(Grabs him by the shoulders.)

Listen, I'm about to drop a brick of truth on you, brother. You are not capable of raising this baby without Ted.

KEVIN. But I'll have you. It'll be you and me. And Lottie makes three.

DONNA. Are you crazy? With what money? Living out of our van?

KEVIN. It'll be an adventure!

DONNA. This is not an adventure, you asshole, this is real life and trust me, you can't handle it!

KEVIN. I'm just as tough as you! We come from the same place. We're from pioneer stack. Stock. We're from a stack of pioneers.

DONNA. *(Grabs ahold of him.)* Listen to me, Kevin. Listen to the sound of my voice. This is what's gonna happen next. You're gonna fix things with Ted, you're gonna take this baby and that is the end of the story!

KEVIN. He won't go for it. But I will. We'll raise it together, we'll figure out a way. You and me.

DONNA. You don't know what it's like not to have money, Kevin. You think it's fun having to give hand jobs just so Lottie can get her teeth cleaned?

KEVIN. Whoa. Don't say that. I don't want to hear stuff like that.

DONNA. Of course you don't, because you've been too busy living in a dainty little fairy bubble! Everything has always been so easy for you! All you have to do is flash your dimples and say something cute and this homo American dream comes raining down on you. You're a complete idiot if you walk away from all of this. And you're not screwing this up for me or this baby!

KEVIN. I told you. It's over. There is no universe where Ted and I change diapers and pick out kindergartens. Forget that universe. It only exists in your head now. It's a ghost planet. But, hey. Don't look so worried. I'm gonna help you out.

(He hugs her.)

You got me.

DONNA. Just tell me one thing, Kevin. You're sure about this? You're not just being rash?

KEVIN. I'm not being rash.

DONNA. Oh, God. We're doomed.

(The lights fade.)

Scene Four

(The next day. Suitcases wait in the living room. **TED** *is on the phone.)*

TED. Yeah, it's almost done. Kevin's doing a really great job on it, too. He just wants a couple more minutes to look it over. He's a perfectionist. And, listen, thank you so much for asking him. And thanks for letting me bring Lottie over the other day. Sorry if things got weird. No, no, it's fine.

*(***KEVIN*** enters with another suitcase.)*

Hey, Anne, let me call you back, okay? Sure. Bye.

(Hangs up, turns to **KEVIN**.*)*

You're being ridiculous. You're being…you're not really going anywhere.

KEVIN. Uh-huh.

TED. Look, Kevin, I'm sorry, okay? I just, I went overboard.

KEVIN. This is just so…sad.

TED. Then make it not sad. I'm sorry. I apologize. We can figure this whole thing out. Don't let your sister screw everything up. She's clearly just some kind of sadist who enjoys dismantling things.

*(***LOTTIE*** enters from the front door. Picks up one of the suitcases and exits. They are silent until she leaves the room.)*

You can't seriously tell me you're going to take off with them. That's completely crazy, baby.

KEVIN. Why? I thought you said I was incapable of taking care of myself, let alone someone else. Might as well, you know, try.

TED. Please don't do this. I'm begging you. Everything was perfect before they got here. She's probably just trying to shake us down for money. I guarantee you that's what it is!

*(***KEVIN*** heads back upstairs.)*

TED. Kevin. Kevin!

*(**DONNA** enters from the kitchen.)*

This is all your fault.

DONNA. *(Frantic, worried)* Yeah, yeah, shut up, I know. I'm trying to rectify this cluster fuck of a situation, okay? You think this is what I wanted? Now I'm gonna have three kids to take care of.

TED. You planted this seed in his head.

DONNA. No, Ted. I'm not that powerful, okay? Whether you like it or not, there's a big gaping hole in Kevin's life.

*(**LOTTIE** enters, unseen.)*

Just say yes to him. I'll stay here for a few months. Not here, but someplace close by and cheap. I'm sure Sag Harbor has a Howard Johnson's or something. And then after the baby comes, Lottie and me, we'll be on our way to the Caribbean or Alaska. I'll sing "Besame Mucho" to fat Americans, Lottie will get to see the world and eat buffet style shrimp. Our life will be all shuffleboard and ice sculptures. And as for you? You'll hire a nanny, it won't be so hard. And those scrapbooks of yours! They'll finally come to life, man! You'll have a little girl to eat your stained-glass gingerbread houses! Instead of going to the movies on Christmas, you'll be waiting for Santa! Think of the birthday parties and the cakes and the letters from camp and the dance recitals! Just say yes, Ted! Why are you fighting it?

TED. It's not that I'm fighting it. Believe me. I've tried to imagine saying yes all night long. But it's just something I can't do. I just can't…

DONNA. Well, then you lose Kevin. He wants a family and if you can't…

LOTTIE. *(Steps forward, urgently.)* I could stay.

DONNA. What?

LOTTIE. If Uncle Kevin wants to have a family, I could stay. Please, please, let me stay. Take me. It'll be easier than

having a baby. It'll only be just for a few years. If it's
money you're worried about, I'll work. I'll get a job…

DONNA. Are you out of your Goddamn mind? I'm not
leaving you here!

LOTTIE. *(Ignores her.)* Don't make me go with her. I'll
runaway if you do. I can't handle her anymore. I can't.
I don't care if you have to call child services, I'll go live
with morbidly obese people. I'll learn to deal with the
smell. I don't care what I have to do, I'm not getting
in that van.

DONNA. You most certainly are, young lady. Besides, what
makes you think they'd want to keep you? Kevin wants
a baby, someone he can raise. He wants a clean slate.
You're coming with me.

LOTTIE. I'll kill myself. I'll jump out of the passenger seat
while we're speeding down the highway. I'll drink
antifreeze.

DONNA. Drama queen, I swear to God.

LOTTIE. Ted! Please!

TED. I…listen, Lottie…

DONNA. See! He doesn't want you. I'm the only one that
wants you. Now stop embarrassing yourself.

LOTTIE. *(Finally turns to* **DONNA.***)* I want out. It's that simple.
I can't raise you anymore.

DONNA. You're hilarious, you know that. You have no idea
the kind of sacrifices I've had to make.

LOTTIE. Then stop making them.

(Turns to **TED.***)*

I called my dad. He blew me off. Told me to never call
him again.

DONNA. I told you, I'm the only one that wants you! I'm
the only one!

LOTTIE. You don't have to pay for school, for food,
anything. I'll figure something out. I promise. I swear
to you. If I can just stay here until…

TED. Lottie, stop. It's okay. If you're sure this is what you really want, then…okay. You can stay with us.

LOTTIE. What?

(She hugs him desperately.)

Oh my God! Thank you! Thank you!! Please don't change your mind!

*(***TED*** is unsure, but hugs her back.)*

DONNA. No, no, no, no, no. I'm not giving up my rights as a mother. I have parental rights!

TED. You were willing to give up rights to your baby.

DONNA. That's different. Oh, any idiot can see how that's different!

*(To **LOTTIE**.)*

You're the world to me, baby. You know that. I can't get by without you.

LOTTIE. Learn!

DONNA. This is not happening. I have rights!

TED. When you wanted us to take your baby, you must have had some sort of price in mind. There must have been some cash settlement.

DONNA. I was trying to help my brother out, that's all. And give my baby a better life.

(Pause.)

But while we're on the subject, I would like to point out that if you and Kevin were to hire a surrogate mother, it would cost you way more.

TED. Way more than what? Way more than what? I thought there wasn't a price tag, Donna.

(She is silent.)

Or I could just see to it that you get hit with a child endangerment case. It would be so easy, not to mention so completely gratifying. All I have to do is make a few calls…

DONNA. Wow. You're actually threatening me?

TED. Very good, Donna. A +.

(*Goes to the desk, takes out a checkbook.*)

How much? A surrogate mother would cost us, I don't know, fifteen thousand? Twenty thousand? I'll give you the same amount to leave Lottie here and never bother us again.

DONNA. Stop it. Leave Lottie out of this!

TED. Come on, Donna. Time's running out. You've got a baby to think of. With business the way it is, I shouldn't be spending this kind of money right now, so don't let me change my mind.

DONNA. Oh, yeah, like you're so hard up.

LOTTIE. You don't know anything about it.

TED. $25,000 and that's my final offer.

DONNA. Oh, fuck you.

LOTTIE. Thirty. Offer her thirty.

TED. What?

LOTTIE. She won't say no to thirty. She can't.

TED. (*Writes out the check.*) I'll make it thirty-five. But you go. And you don't come back unless Lottie calls you.

(*He holds the check out.* **DONNA** *stares at him.*)

Well?

DONNA. (*To* **LOTTIE.**) This isn't what I wanted.

LOTTIE. It's what I want.

(**DONNA** *hesitates.*)

It's what I want!

(**DONNA** *still hesitates.*)

You don't have to pretend you don't want the check, mom. I can see you already spending it in your head. Just save some for the baby and you'll be fine. You know I'll be better off here. Tell me I wouldn't be better off if I stayed. It won't be forever. Just a couple of years. Think of it as if I'm going away to camp or something.

(**DONNA** *looks away.*)

LOTTIE. I need to be still. I just want to be still for a while.

DONNA. I can come and visit, right? I mean, you don't hate me that much?

TED. If and when Lottie calls you.

DONNA. *(Shakes her head, but slowly takes the check.)* Fine. You win. Congratulations. You both win.

> *(***KEVIN** *enters and* **DONNA** *quickly stashes the check.)*

You ready to go, Kevin?

TED. He's staying here.

DONNA. No, he's not.

KEVIN. No, I'm not.

TED. Everything's changed. Lottie's going to stay with us.

KEVIN. That's good. That's the best idea I've heard all day.

> *(To* **LOTTIE.** *)*

Sorry we ruined your un-birthday.

> *(To* **DONNA.** *)*

You wanna grab those bags? Traffic is going to get nasty the longer we wait.

DONNA. You're the boss.

> *(***DONNA** *turns to* **LOTTIE.** *Goes to hug her,* **LOTTIE** *receives it coldly.* **DONNA** *pulls away.)*

So. Whatever happened to Lily?

LOTTIE. Who?

DONNA. The hat maker. The one in your book. The one who wouldn't settle down. Did things turn out okay for her?

LOTTIE. She…yeah. Things turned out really great. She meets the perfect guy and everything turns out fine.

DONNA. So, you're sure it's got a happy ending and everything?

LOTTIE. Of course. It's called "The House of Mirth", isn't it?

DONNA. Well, good. I'm glad.

(**DONNA** *exits.* **LOTTIE** *turns to* **KEVIN**.)

LOTTIE. Don't let her raise that baby in a van.

KEVIN. I'm on it.

(**LOTTIE** *nods, moves upstage.*)

TED. But, Kevin. Lottie's staying. Everything's changed. Isn't this what you wanted? I mean, a version of what you wanted? I don't know what else I can...

KEVIN. No, it's great. You and Lottie? I can't think of anything more perfect. But you...wait, how does Donna put it? You dropped a brick of truth on me last night.

TED. Can we please just act like that never happened?

KEVIN. But it did. And it's okay. The book is shit and I need to figure out how to not be an emotional fourteen year old anymore. And besides, Donna can't do this thing on her own. She's Donna. She needs me.

TED. I need you. I do.

KEVIN. That's the thing, Ted. You don't need anything. You never have.

(**KEVIN** *embraces* **TED**, *then exits.* **LOTTIE** *and* **TED** *stare at one another. Lights up on* **DONNA** *driving the van and* **KEVIN** *riding shotgun.*)

DONNA. Jesus.

KEVIN. What?

DONNA. He should have just bought you that fucking dog.

KEVIN. Things are about to get real, aren't they?

(**LOTTIE** *and* **TED** *stand silently. The phone rings.* **TED** *goes and answers it.*)

TED. Hello? Oh, hey, Anne. Oh, yeah, sorry about that. I'll email it over right now. Uh-huh. Sure. Okay then. Bye.

(**TED** *slowly walks over to the computer, sits down and starts typing.* **LOTTIE** *slowly walks over to him. She reads over his shoulder.*)

LOTTIE. The curbstones were fashioned out of the ballasts of ancient whaling ships that frequented the port...

(Pause. **TED** *stops typing.)*

Maybe you could talk about the literary influences. Compare the Sag Harbor of today with how it was when Steinbeck roamed the streets.

*(***TED*** *starts to cry.)*

LOTTIE. Move over. Seriously, move over.

*(***TED*** *does,* **LOTTIE** *starts to type. Lights up on* **KEVIN** *and* **DONNA** *in the van. They drive silently for a moment.)*

DONNA. Kevin?

KEVIN. Yeah?

DONNA. What the hell are we gonna do now?

*(***KEVIN*** *reaches over and puts his hand on* **DONNA***'s stomach.)*

KEVIN. *(Solemnly, but still with a slight southern accent.)* Young lady, what have I told you about acting up in front of company?

DONNA. *(Pause, then...)* Where, pray tell, are your pantyhose?

KEVIN & DONNA. That is not the proper way to use an oyster fork!

(They smile, then look unsure. **LOTTIE** *turns to* **TED***.)*

LOTTIE. Read this. How's this?

TED. Good. It's very good.

(Lights fade)

End of Play